Girl's Pixie Costume

Use good-quality satin, and tulle netting for wings

For my Val

First edition 2015

Library of Congress Catalog Card Number 2013957482
ISBN 978-0-7636-6111-3

15 16 17 18 19 20 CCP 10 9 8 7 6 5 4 3 2 1

Printed in Shenzhen, Guangdong, China

This book was typeset in Maiandra.
The illustrations were done in watercolor and aquarelle pencil.

Candlewick Press
99 Dover Street
Somerville, Massachusetts 02144

visit us at www.candlewick.com

JJ
WELLS
ROSEMARY

FELIX
STANDS TALL

ROSEMARY WELLS

CANDLEWICK PRESS

"Felix," said Fiona, "do you have a best friend?"

"No," said Felix. "I don't have a best friend."

"Can I be your best friend?" asked Fiona.

"I would love that," said Felix.

"That's settled, then," said Fiona. "Now we'll be in the big talent show."

"We will?" asked Felix.

"It's easy," said Fiona. "We're going to win first prize!'

"We are?" asked Felix.

Fiona said, "We'll sing 'There's a Pixie in My Garden.'"

"Do we have to?" asked Felix.

"Best friends do everything together!" said Fiona.

Felix did not want to lose his best friend.

So he told his mama he wanted to be a pixie for the talent show at the Guinea Pig Jubilee.

Felix's mama got out her sewing box.

Snip, *snip* went her scissors.

Zizz, *zizz* went her sewing machine.

Pretty soon Felix had a pixie hat, green shorts, and turned-up-toe shoes.

Fiona was all ready for Felix.

"Now we have to practice," she said.

Fiona taught Felix to sing "There's a Pixie in My Garden."

Then she taught him the Texas slide step

and how to line-dance in costume.

Many amazing acts lit up the big show.

But when it came time for the audience to vote,
it was Pixies in the Garden all the way to first prize.

Felix's heart swelled with pride.

And that's when the trouble started.

Minkie, Bucky, and Dimples were waiting for Felix in the school yard.

"Here comes Twinkletoes!" they shouted.

Bucky sang "There's a Pixie in My Soup."

Dimples made fun of Felix's Texas slide step.

And Minkie put a Slime Creeper down Felix's shirt.

Felix ran home as fast as he could.

"What happened to my angel boy?" asked
Felix's mama.

Felix told her about Minkie, Bucky, Dimples,
and the Slime Creeper.

"Felix, my angel, you are going to have to
stand tall," said Felix's mama.

But Felix didn't know how to stand tall.

Minkie tied Felix's
gym shoes together.

"Shall we dance?" sang Dimples.

Bucky put a chirping plastic cricket
in Felix's egg-salad sandwich.

"Felix, you are a hot mess!" said Fiona
at lunchtime.

Felix didn't want to be a hot mess.

"Watch me!" said Fiona.

Fiona stared down Dimples, Bucky, and Minkie until they slinked away.

"I could never do that," said Felix.

"I'm wearing a Magic Protection Suit," said Fiona.

"I don't see anything," said Felix.

"It's invisible," said Fiona. "I have an extra."

At Fiona's house, Fiona gave Felix her extra
Magic Protection Suit.

"Go ahead! Put it on!" she said.

The armor was as light as a feather but strong.

"You look so brave, Felix!" said Fiona.

"I do?" said Felix. And suddenly Felix felt brave.

On the way to school the next day, Felix stood tall and proud in his Magic Protection Suit.

The morning sunlight faded the silvery steel to near invisible. It didn't matter one bit.

"Here comes Mr. Pixie Pants!" giggled Dimples.

"Take that back!" said Felix.

Felix glared at Minkie, Bucky, and Dimples through his invisible visor.

Clang! went his invisible lance on the sidewalk.

Whap! went his invisible gauntlets.

The troublemakers melted away like snow.

Felix couldn't wait to tell Fiona.

But before he could say a word, Fiona said,
"Oh, Felix! How about wearing twin cupcake
costumes for the Halloween parade?"

Felix knew he had to stand tall again.

"How about being fire-breathing dragons?"
said Felix.

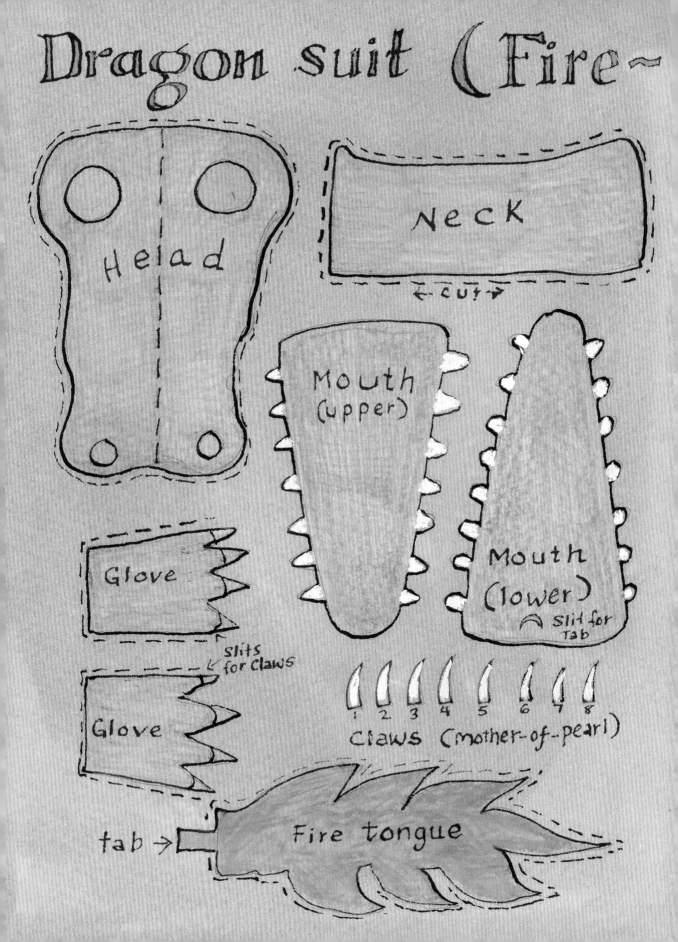